Up
in the Attic

A Story ABC

BY HILDA K. WILLIAMS

PICTURES BY CORINNE MALVERN

SIMON AND SCHUSTER · NEW YORK

THE LITTLE GOLDEN BOOKS ARE PREPARED UNDER THE SUPERVISION OF

MARY REED, Ph.D.

FORMERLY OF TEACHERS COLLEGE, COLUMBIA UNIVERSITY

To

DAVY-BILL and FRITZIE-ANNE

Author and Artist

Hilda K. Williams is a native Iowan and still retains her western accent, although she lives in Bucks County, Pennsylvania. Miss Williams is a specialist in children's reading and primary books.

Corinne Malvern has excelled in two of the arts. She was a successful child actress, then studied art, and has since exhibited her work and done commercial art. Among the books she has illustrated are THE GOLDEN CHRISTMAS BOOK and the Little Golden Books, NURSERY SONGS, COUNTING RHYMES, CHRISTMAS CAROLS, HYMNS, POETRY and SINGING GAMES.

This is an **attic,** old and gray,
Where hundreds of things are tucked away —
    Just as they are in your attic.

And here is a **boy**—his name is Ted.
One night, when he ought to have been in bed,
He went instead to the attic.

The **clock** in the hall was old and slow.
"Tick, tock!" it said. "No, Ted, don't go!
You can't go to bed in the attic!"

D

A little **dog**—he was only a pup—
Saw the boy go and followed him up,
When Ted went up to the attic.

One **ear** up and one ear down!
The little dog really was quite a clown,
As he raced upstairs to the attic.

F

A **flashlight** lay by the attic door.
The little dog rolled it over the floor,
And into the dusky attic.

G

Ted waved the flashlight and looked around.
"Oh, look!" he cried. "Just see what I found!
My little old **gun** in the attic!"

H

Beside an old **hat** hanging low on a rack
Was a feather **headdress,** red and black.
Now who put that in the attic?

I

"I'll be an **Indian** chief," said Ted,
As he painted his cheeks with Indian red.
"We'll camp right here in the attic."

J

He gave a **jump,** and the dog jumped, too,
For that is the way that Indians do
When they camp at night in an attic.

K

"A **kettle!**" cried Ted. "It's not very new,
But just the thing for an Indian stew,
   If we kill a bear in the attic!"

L

He **laughed** as he hung up the kettle, and then
All at once he was laughing again.
He'd found something else in the attic.

M

Masks for Ted and the puppy, too!
I really don't like these things, do you?
Not even for play in the attic!

N

Then Ted found a **nose** that was long and red.
He slipped the strings right over his head.
What a terrible sight for an attic!

An old **owl** stared with a glassy eye
To see if the dog and boy would try
To disturb his peace in the attic.

P

From his **perch** on high the queer-looking bird
Peered down in silence. You could have heard
A little pin drop in the attic.

Ted grabbed a **quilt.** "I'll use this," he said,
"And throw it over the big owl's head.
We'll cook this bird in the attic."

R

Down came the owl on top of Ted,
And he spilled some paint—a brilliant **red**.
What a mess that was in the attic!

S

Then a frightened **squirrel** as big as a cat
Went flying across the room like a bat—
What a sight to see in an attic!

T

The little dog wagged his **tail** for joy.
Away went the dog, and away went the boy,
As the squirrel raced through the attic.

Behind an **umbrella** the squirrel fled—
It fell to the floor, and so did Ted,
    While the squirrel skipped out of the attic.

V

A **valentine** lay there lost on the floor
Where someone had dropped it years before
In that dusty, rubbishy attic.

Under the **window** the valentine lay.
Ted ran to get it—then backed away.
He saw something queer in the attic.

X marks the mirror—you see it, too.
Now what do you think a boy should do,
If he saw such a face in the attic?

Y

"**Yipee!**" cried Ted. "I'm going away.
I was sent to bed, and I heard the clock say
I shouldn't come to this attic!"

Zipp-zipp! Ted went by the quickest route.
The little dog followed in hot pursuit,
   And they tumbled out of the attic.

Dad heard the tumble as well as the shout,
And he and Mother came rushing out
    To see what was wrong in the attic.

"Oh, Mother!" cried Dad. "What's this I see?
A terrible Indian looking at me,
And I think he came from our attic!"

"It's not an Indian at all!" cried Ted.
"It's your little boy, who started to bed
    And then went up to the attic!

"But if you want to see something bad,
Just come with me!" So Mother and Dad
And Ted went back to the attic.

Ted looked at the mirror and gave a sigh.
"Oh, Daddy!" he said. "It was only I—
 The thing I saw in the attic!"

He went to bed—you know it was time—
And that is the end of this alphabet rhyme
And the Indian pranks in the attic.